BRADY

A NOVELLA

D.W. HITZ

BRADY
© 2021 D.W. Hitz

ISBN-13 (Digital): 978-1-956492-11-8
ISBN-13 (Paperback): 978-1-956492-12-5

Edited by *Richard T. Ryan*
Cover Design by *Evan Scale*
Interior Design by D.*W. Hitz*

www.FedowarPress.com
Fedowar Press, LLC

Books from D.W. Hitz

Adult Fiction
Judith's Prophecy (Big Sky Terror Book 1)
Judith's Blood (Big Sky Terror Book 2)
Judith's Fall (Big Sky Terror Book 3)
Gods are Born

Middle Grade Fiction
They Stole the Earth!
The Curse of Grohl

Contributions to Anthologies
Star Crossed
Bounties, Beasts, and Badlands
Remnants: Volume One
Fedowar Holiday Horrors: Volume One

CHAPTER ONE

The sun cast an orange light on the front door as Karl Chambers grabbed the knob. His shoulder ached as he turned his wrist, and a sigh escaped his lips. He spread the door wide into an empty home.

It wasn't empty of furniture; it was empty of life, and the lack of companionship weighed on his chest. The absence of claws clacking against the wood floor. The quiet. Without panting, without a shallow whine from Brady being excited he was home. It was empty of the love he felt at every re-entry.

His breath trembled as he shut the door. He took a seat on the bench that separated the entry from the living room and removed his boots. He checked their soles and found they had much less dirt clumped between the treads than he had expected. He had already wiped away the blood. He set them aside.

The silence permeated his being. The corners of his eyes burned. Brady was gone, the shot still ringing in his ears. He could still feel the last touch, the last time his fingers would stroke the thick black fur. His stomach was sour.

His gaze passed over a pair of small purple hiking boots by the wall, and he thought about how Amanda's face would look when she came to visit in a few days. The tears. The hugs of grief. He would have to tell her about it, and it would ruin at least the first day of her visit, maybe all of it.

Karl stood and walked across the living room, through the kitchen, and paused in the laundry room long enough to strip his clothes away and drop them into the washer. He wanted the dirt, the essence of what he had done, all of it, washed away as soon as possible. He stood naked and poured in detergent, then entered his room.

The shower rinsed away his sweat and soothed his muscles. His shoulders still hurt from digging the grave, and he imagined they would continue to for days, if not a week. He had to make the hole deep. This was the country, and if he didn't dig deep, a bear or fox or even a mountain lion might dig up the body and eat it. The smell would call them, even through several feet of dirt. Brady deserved better than that. And Karl felt that he deserved whatever pain he had been forced to go through for doing the job.

Whether or not the event was Karl's fault was debatable, but he blamed himself. He knew Brady was aggressive when he got off the property. He knew if Brady got out of the house without being on a leash, the dog would run and run, no matter who tried to call him back. He blamed it on the hound in his ancestry. The Lab made him big; the hound made him run and chase. He had known that at some point, Brady was going to get loose and cause a problem. He'd been told by the neighbors, told by his friends, told by anyone who had met the dog that it was a problem waiting to happen. "One day, he's going to bite a kid, and you'll get sued," his brother had told him.

At least it wasn't a kid, Karl thought.

Karl pictured the large black dog, his giant brown eyes shining with love. He remembered the smell of gunsmoke and aspirated blood. He didn't want to do it. But after Brady bit that old woman–either he or Animal Control would have to do it, and Brady was *his* dog, *his* responsibility. So he did what he had to do. And he'd hate himself every day for the rest of his life for having to do it.

Karl turned off the water and dried himself. He went into the kitchen–near dark from the onset of night–and took a can of beer from the fridge. There were five in there, and Karl figured they'd all be gone by the time he hit the sheets that night.

He sat in his gray recliner and felt around on the end table for the remote. He clicked the television on and reclined. He popped open the can and flipped through the menu on Hulu.

There were a thousand things to watch, and he cared about none of them. Each thumbnail caused a feeling of exhaustion. The thought of watching any of them made him shrink at the idea of having to pay attention to something. His mind wasn't ready for that. No, he needed something thoughtless, something he had seen a thousand times and required no active thought, something he could turn on and ignore.

Karl guzzled his beer for a solid thirty seconds and flipped the Roku over to Vudu. He scanned the movies in his library and chose *Airplane!*, a mindless gap-filler, something that would occupy the quiet in his home long enough for him to swallow a few beers and hopefully prepare him to pass out. He wanted to pass out. He dared not go to bed, though, or he'd spend the next two hours rolling back and forth, unable to sleep, picturing Brady's grave being filled in with clumps of dirt and clay, shovelful by shovelful.

He guzzled again. The movie started.

There was only darkness when it happened. Only quiet. The movie had finished. Karl's eyes were shut. His mind was in some other place, a realm of sleep not far from the surface, but enough for him to have forgotten the truths of the real world.

Beer cans had gathered on the end table. Karl's recliner was up, and a light blanket had found its way onto his legs at some point. That was when something made itself known.

Brang, brang, brang, rising twangs shouted through the room from behind Karl. They rang like the rising pitch on a discordant acoustic guitar. But it was too loud for a guitar. And Karl had no guitar. And even if he did, there was no one else in the house to play it.

Karl shot up in his seat, eyes wide. Chills ran through him. He spun, staring into the kitchen, the dining room.

"What the hell was that?"

He saw little. The television was a wall of black, and the dim glow it emitted merely lit the surrounding few feet. And those few feet weren't where the noise had come from. It had come from the dining room.

Karl lowered the recliner and stood. He felt a chill. He must have left the windows open, and the night's breeze was creeping through the house. He was sure that was it. That was the cause of the noise–of course–the change in temperature and the house settling.

He wasn't convinced. The coolness in his veins spread.

He squinted through the open concept space into the dining room. There was nothing in there that could have made that sound. A table, some chairs, the antique china cabinet, all of which he had inherited from his mother with the house.

"Is someone there?"

There was no answer. And why should there be? Karl fought back his shivers, convincing himself he was being ridiculous. There had been no noise. He had been sleeping and had a dream of someone twanging an old guitar–that was all. Then, he woke up, depressed about Brady, and he imagined something. That type of thing was supposed to happen to people who were sad, wasn't it?

Karl rubbed his arms, shook his head. He picked up the remote and clicked the television off. It was time for bed.

He crossed the living room to close the dining room windows. His gaze went to the spot in front of the china cabinet where Brady often laid. In the darkness, he saw him. The shadowy silhouette of a large black dog was there, and Karl gasped.

He stopped and gulped. He took a step closer. It was gone, nothing, a trick of the light.

It was late; he was drunk; he felt guilty; his mind was playing tricks on him; he told himself all of those things and brushed away the pins and needles that were tickling his skin.

Karl walked to the sliding door and locked it. He pictured Brady standing outside, staring up at him, waiting to come in. Karl's eyes burned. He turned and went to bed.

When morning came and the rays of daylight broke through the bedroom curtains, Karl was relieved. His head ached, his entire body was sore, and he was drop-dead tired, but it was a new day. A day without Brady, which he hated, but an end to a sleepless, unrestful state.

He rolled to the edge of the bed and hung his feet down to the floor. Squeaks of his mattress reminded him of something he'd heard overnight, a high-pitched sound from the living area and clunks and cracks of the house settling. The house did that during the spring and fall, days where the temperature swung greatly between hot and cold. But last night there were too many. Too many noises. And it couldn't have been as loud and as long as it seemed. It must have been a dream. One of those things the mind amplifies inside itself, a recurring echo as the subconscious tries to figure out a mystery.

Karl pushed to his feet and dragged himself to the bathroom. As he stood in front of the toilet, aiming into the bowl, Karl felt as though something were watching him. He glanced around the room, half-expecting to see Brady in the doorway, waiting to be served his breakfast. Nothing. He shook his head and drained his bladder.

He wondered if the entire day would be like this. Constant remembrances of his beloved pet. Of his betrayal of a friend.

In the kitchen, Karl opened the refrigerator door. He expected to hear the clack of claws race across the house. It didn't happen.

He cooked sausage and eggs and made a cup of coffee. It was only when he sat at the counter to eat that Karl's gaze passed into the dining room and over the china cabinet.

"What the fuck?" He dropped his food on the counter and stared. The clank of his ceramic plate against the brown laminate surface went unnoticed.

Across the dining room were scattered each and every dish that had been in the cabinet when Karl went to sleep. The china, like the cabinet itself, was all inherited from his mother because he had no sister to take them, and his brother didn't care. Mom had left it with him along with the house, hoping he might give it to Amanda one day.

The stuff was plain and inelegant compared to the high-priced tableware of today, and he doubted that it was the type a young woman would want by the time she was old enough to receive it. But he also would have doubted that he would have woken up to see this.

Bowls, plates, and teacups covered the table, chairs, and floor. Blue on white swirls and roses made a collage of round shapes across the dining room. Few things appeared broken, but each dish and cup was stacked haphazardly on top of one another, off-kilter and on-edge, as if the slightest nudge might send the entirety down to the floor in a crash.

"What the fuck?" Karl repeated.

He walked slowly around the counter.

"What could have done this?" It couldn't have been an earthquake. That may have knocked the cabinet over but not lifted the contents out and dropped them on the table. Did someone break-in during the night? It wasn't a concern that ever bothered him before. Brady was such a good guardian; if anyone had come in, they would have wished they hadn't–but Brady wasn't there last night.

Karl glanced at the television–still there; it wasn't a burglary. He took a walk around the house, checking doors and windows. All locked, just as he had left them. The only thing out of place was the dining room. He walked around the outside of the dining table–stepping where he could without destroying plates, saucers, and cups. The spot on the floor where Brady would have lain was strangely clear of debris.

Karl kneeled and touched the spot. It was warmer than he expected, and a cold chill crossed the back of his neck. He shivered and looked up at the cabinet.

The old oak was carved in a style he had been told was French country. It was generally plain on the top half, but the bottom had ornate flourishes and details that always struck him as odd. Symbols were carved into the wood in a way that made them look like decoration but stood out to Karl as being out of place–as intentional but veiled.

As his gaze passed the windowless lower half, something inside caught his eye. There was a dark thing, nearly black, in the middle of the cabinet. It wasn't on the shelf, though; it looked like it was stuck to the ceiling, above the molding and recessed upward, where no one could possibly see it without getting down low–and probably not without emptying the cabinet first.

Karl reached for it. The air within the cabinet was frigid. It was like the inside of a freezer on a hot day; it made the hairs on his arms stand up and stiffen.

In the hard-to-see crevice, Karl felt something smooth, like a velvety cloth. It was wrapped around a hard, circular object no wider than Karl's hand. He gripped it with his thumb and pinky and pulled. The thing seemed to peel away like a strip of Velcro.

"What is this?" He scooted back from the mess and stared at the thing in his hand. The velvety cloth was a bag with a folded end. He found the opening and tipped it upside down, letting the contents fall into his free hand.

The object that fell was cool and gray, round and smooth like a stone disc. Karl's hand felt the coolness creep over his skin and into his fingers.

He flipped the disc and examined the other side. This side wasn't smooth and blank; it was intricately carved. Interconnected circles and strange pictures decorated the disc. They looked hieroglyphic but not Egyptian. Brown stains overlapped the carvings, and a deep sense of dread sank into Karl as he traced them with his finger.

Numbness moved down Karl's digits and into his palm. He flipped the disc over and moved it from hand to hand, trying to see what was causing the sensation. He saw nothing, but the feeling drifted from hand to hand, following the stone circle, until both his hands felt numb from palms to fingertips.

"Shit." Karl dropped it on the floor. It wobbled and clunked on the wood. He shuffled backward, staring the circle down as he moved. He looked at his hands, hoping the numbness would abate, but something called his eyes back to the disc. Something called him to move forward, closer to the strange thing.

Karl couldn't feel his fingers, but still, he reached to touch it. Something told him to keep going that the strange feeling would pass. He just had to pick the stone circle up, and everything would be all right.

He placed his hand over it, again with his thumb and pinky on its edges. He lifted it and held it in front of his face. He forced himself to look away and then back because what he saw didn't make any sense. It wasn't right, but it held wonder. The carvings in the stone; they were moving. The strange words, the drawings; they were rotating, sliding, shifting over and under each other.

It was too weird. A sight such as he had never seen before.

Wonder turned to worry. Worry turned to fear. Karl attempted to put the disc back down, but when he tried to let go, his fingers wouldn't release. Instead, the cold numbness moved up his arms. It moved over his chest. The freezing sensation flowed down to his legs.

Karl tried to scream. His mouth refused to move. As the numbness rose up his neck, a warm wetness rolled down. It came from above his forehead, over his face like a baptism. But it wasn't warm water. What he saw come over his eyes like a sheet was blood.

Chapter Two

When Karl opened his eyes, it was dark. His fingers were wet, sticky, and the muscles in his hands hurt. He was lying on the floor and pushed himself into a sitting position. His back ached, as did his arms and legs. Was this all from digging? It could have been, but something told him there was more to it. He was dizzy, and he knew that if the room were lit, it would be spinning around him.

The faint light from below the microwave lit Karl's hand as he held it up. He groaned and rubbed his fingers together. They were almost black in the gloom, and he could smell them now. The dark stickiness was blood.

"What happened?" Karl's eyes widened. Had he hurt himself? Was he bleeding? He began patting himself down from head to toe. No wounds, or at least he couldn't find any. Only the ache of whatever he'd done to himself since... He thought back and remembered. *This morning?*

Karl stood up and flipped on the light. What had he been doing since this morning? His breakfast sat on the counter right where he'd left it. His mother's china was not.

Across the table, the chairs, the dining room floor, were thousands of chunks of broken porcelain. Karl's mouth dropped. The dark hardwood looked white from shattered remains–except for one spot, Brady's spot.

Karl braced his head with his hands, forgetting the layer of sticky blood until it was pressed into his hair. His fingertips and hair clung to each other and pinched at his scalp.

"Ew," Karl groaned and pulled his hands back. His hair puffed out as he removed them. Strands formed points from the wetness. Drops polka-dotted his cheekbones and forehead.

Fear gripped Karl's thoughts. If it weren't from him, where was the blood from? Who *was* hurt? And was *he* responsible?

Blue lights flashed through the living room window. They raced across the dining room wall, then did it again as if running laps.

Police.

Karl froze, images of blue lights from five years ago flooding his thoughts. He shook them away as his mind dug through his memory, searching for any crumbs of what had happened–of what he'd done. He found nothing. He wondered if he had head trauma. Or was he blocking something out?

He ran to the window. Two state troopers had stopped in front of the Mertzs' place across the street. They stood in front of an open front door, and an officer was shining his light inside. The other turned and vomited on the lawn.

Karl looked at his hands, burgundy in the police strobe. "Oh, my god."

Had he done something to Hank? Reba?

Pictures cycled through Karl's mind. Reba's bloody arm after Brady had bitten her. The arguments over the dog. Karl had promised to pay her medical bills, but it wasn't enough for the Mertzs.

"Put him down," Hank had said. "Put him down, and we won't sue. Other than that, we got trouble."

So he did. But Karl had no idea how many people Hank had told the story to. And if something bad happened to the Mertzs now–the way it looked through the window–the police would surely be over to talk to Karl soon whether he were involved or not.

Karl tore across the house and started his shower. He saw himself in the mirror and trembled. A layer of red coated his skin from head to foot. Coated his clothes. Whatever had happened between the morning and night was something he didn't want to remember. And, God, what if it really were his fault? Whatever had occurred across the street, it was looking more and more likely that he may have had something to do with it.

It occurred to Karl that with as much blood as was on him, it may be around his house as well. Evidence of whatever had happened. Evidence that may send him back to prison.

While the shower heated, he went back to the dining room. Small pools of red were on the floor where he had woken up. Drops of blood trailed from there to the front door.

"Fuck," Karl exhaled the word with disgust.

He ran to the kitchen, grabbed 409, paper towels, and plastic grocery bags. He frantically scrubbed the floor, clearing away the pools, the drops, anything he could, and shoved the dirty towels into the plastic bags. It wasn't perfect–likely wouldn't stand up to a *CSI* investigation, but he could clean it better later. At least if those troopers came into the house, it would stand up to a cursory inspection.

Karl put the bags in his bathroom closet. He stripped off his clothes, put them in another bag, and threw them in the closet as well. He pushed the closet door shut, and as if by its own will, the stone disc jumped from the bag with his clothes and rolled across the floor.

"No, no, no," Karl said. He shoved it back into the closet with his toe and shut the door. Then, he jumped in the shower.

Karl's skin stung as he dressed. He had never scrubbed himself so hard. He had just made it to the kitchen, body still on the edge of damp, the last beer in his hand and ready to open, when a knock came to the front door.

Shit. His hands trembled. He cracked open the can of beer and guzzled.

Knock, knock, knock.

Shit. He had to get it. They wouldn't go away, and the longer he took to answer, the guiltier he would appear.

"Just a sec!" He guzzled more beer. The can was two-thirds empty now, and his hands had stopped shaking. He walked to the front door.

Officer Mitchell Rucker and Officer Jake Bartram had joined each other when they arrived at the call. Their lights were almost in sync as they rode up the hill to the residence. The 911 report had seemed outlandish at first–an elderly man screaming that his wife had been torn to pieces by some *thing*-but as they walked from their cruisers to the gaping front door, they had each pulled their weapons simultaneously.

Rucker kept his cool, somehow. Bartram tossed his dinner in the bushes. Neither wanted to go inside.

An old man-likely the caller-sat in a chair on the far side of the room. His eyes were glazed over, chest still. Rucker studied what he could see from the door, and his dinner nearly joined Bartram's. The man's gut was sliced from one bottom rib to the other. His intestines bulged through the opening, and Rucker suspected a dark brown mass on the man's right was one edge of his liver. The telephone rested in his hand.

Rucker studied the scene-what he could see of it. Layers of blood and viscera covered nearly the entirety of the room. The ceiling was splattered with liquids of various colors. The furniture dripped with tissue, bile, and blood. The only clues that the second victim was a female were an elderly woman's head on the couch and a dainty, multi-ringed hand that rested on top of the coffee table. The head was on its side. One eye was closed. The other was open. It appeared to be winking, as if teasing, inviting them in.

The smell, which had hit them as soon as their cruiser doors opened, now penetrated Rucker's every thought. It was a mix of iron, shit, and vomit. He shuddered and stumbled backward.

"I'm not going in there," Bartram said. His lip quivered. His gun dipped from the open door. "Besides, look-" He pointed to the carpet. "There's nowhere to walk. We'd be contaminating the scene."

Rucker looked. The carpet was soaked from end to end in blood and whatever else had been inside that poor old woman. There was no way to go in the front door without traipsing through it. But that was no excuse not to do their job.

As he examined the entryway floor, Rucker noticed something else. Dark spots. He took out his flashlight. Red footprints led away from the home, down the driveway, to the street.

"You see this?" Rucker said.

"Yeah," Bartram said, relieved to do anything other than go inside.

"We better see where it leads."

"Could be the killer."

Karl opened his front door and froze. Two .40 caliber Glocks pointed at his face. He opened his mouth to speak, but words failed him.

"Don't move," Officer Rucker said.

Karl couldn't move if he wanted to. His chest pounded. Fear locked his joints in place.

Bartram pushed the door as wide as it would go with his free hand and gazed inside. "Anyone else here?"

Karl shook his head. His eyes remained fixed on the barrels of the officers' guns.

"Put your hands against the door," Bartram said.

"Wha-" Karl stammered.

"Now!" Rucker demanded.

Karl did as he was told. Bartram slammed his face into the metal door and seized his hands. Karl heard the ratcheting sound of cuffs closing around his wrists and felt the pinch of tightened steel. Warm wetness ran over his lips, and he realized his nose was throbbing.

"What the fuck?" Karl shouted.

"You got him?" Rucker asked.

"Yeah." Bartram began searching Karl's pockets.

"I'll clear the home." Rucker walked into the living room. He paused, examining the crushed ceramics in the dining room, and continued on to the kitchen.

Bartram found nothing in Karl's left pocket. He holstered his gun and searched the other pocket. He discovered something large and struggled to pull it out. Karl's pants lifted with each pull until the object slid free.

"What the hell is this?" Bartram asked.

Karl looked over his shoulder. Blood ran onto his lips and dripped from his chin onto his shirt. Bartram was holding the disc.

How? Karl wondered. He didn't remember putting that in his pocket. The last he saw of it, he had shoved it into the bathroom closet.

Bartram flipped it over and saw the carving, the blood. He had barely uttered a syllable of question when the room darkened.

The lights did not dim so much as the space inside the home was removed from the light. A gray essence replaced the room's illumination, and in the center of the living room, a black fog took shape. It was round, barely larger than a person, with swirling strands of smoke that circled away and back into itself. With each rotation of smoke, the room plunged deeper into dread.

Bartram dropped the disc and drew his pistol again. That was all the time needed for the swirl of fog to cross the room.

The thing radiated despair. It washed the room in a sense of impending doom that intensified as it drew closer. It dug in as the lights from this world were consumed and this thing from another place fed.

Bartram shook. His finger barely found the trigger. He raised his hand to aim, and a dozen black tentacles shot from the cloud.

Karl could barely see what was happening. Then Bartram's grip loosened, and he turned his head. He noticed the tentacles were odd; unlike octopus or squid, they bore no suction cups. Instead, they were adorned with thorns, barbs that reminded him of the tips of fishing hooks, meant to penetrate and hold–and never release without tearing the body. At the very ends of the monstrous appendages were claws. And the sight of them unblocked a memory of Reba Mertz's flesh being torn from her body.

"No," Karl whispered. Visions of soaring blood and flesh raced through his mind. Screams. Gaseous mists of hot blood and tears.

All twelve tentacles wrapped around Bartram. They shone in the dim light and oozed black goo. He squeezed the trigger, and a shot tunneled into the floor. Oak splinters exploded upward.

Two tentacles flung away from the officer. He howled as lines of bloody geysers sprayed from his arm and his abdomen. The tentacles soared back into the fog, inch-wide balls of flesh clinging to their barbs.

"Fuck!" Bartram screamed.

A droning ruckus emerged from the fog. It boomed into the living room, wiping away all other sound. Before Karl could wonder what the noise could mean, Bartram was yanked from the doorway. He howled and vanished into the swirling fog.

A scream of tremendous pain tore from the fog as streams of blood and viscera erupted from within. Tissue sprayed across the ceiling, the couch, the recliner, and the dining room furniture. And in a blink, the fog vanished, and light returned.

Karl stared motionless into his home. He raised trembling hands to his face and covered his mouth, then realized his cuffs had been broken. The chain that linked one to the other had been sliced, and two half links rested in the blood pool that flooded from Bartram's remains.

A nervous laugh slipped through Karl's lips. He could feel his heart thumping. Hear it in the silence of the room whose only noise was a series of drips: Officer Bartram's fluids falling from the ceiling, light fixtures, and dining room chandelier.

Karl backed out through the doorway as Officer Rucker entered the room with a plastic bag in hand. Karl recognized it instantly. It was the bag with his bloody clothes.

Rucker stopped. His gaze went to the ceiling, the table, the floor. He dropped the bag and covered his mouth. He looked to the door and raised his pistol at Karl. "Bartram!" He looked at the ceiling, where streaks of stretched and emptied intestines stuck, glued to the plaster. "Jake? Where are you?" His voice was loud, trembling.

"He's gone," Karl muttered.

"Jake?" Rucker crossed the room, maintaining his aim at Karl's chest. "Where is he, you fucking sicko?"

Blood dripped onto Rucker as he walked. Red lines streaked down his cheeks, and points formed in his tightly-cropped, brown hair.

Karl pointed to the ceiling, gestured to the room as a whole. Hunks of fat rolled down the wall behind the television. Splintered bone and ground muscle lay on the table. "He's–he's gone."

"What did you do?" Rucker shouted. He ran toward Karl.

"What did you do?"

The room's lights began to flutter and dim. It was coming back. The thing–whatever it was–was coming back.

Karl backed onto the front porch as the black swirling fog emerged into his living room from whatever place it resided. It drained the light in waves, pulses, as if gulping it down. And this time, it was larger. It was now the width of two people. He wondered: if he could remember what had happened at the Mertzs; would it have gotten bigger from that encounter? Was it growing every time it killed? Or was it–fed?

Officer Rucker reached the doorway and froze. His eyes had been fixed on Karl, but now they were drawn back into the home, back to the thing floating, spinning, winding into itself in rhythmic, hypnotic patterns.

"That's not..." Officer Rucker trailed off. "It can't be."

A dozen black tentacles spread from the cloud, their barbed claws eager. They pointed at the officer, and Rucker stumbled backward.

"No." Rucker shook his head.

Tentacles darted across the room, and Rucker spun and leaped through the front door.

One, two, three tentacles missed. The fourth found Rucker's ankle and ripped his foot backward. The fifth grabbed his other leg as the remainder snapped in the air like whips.

Karl watched, his mouth open. He reached toward the cop and stopped. What could he do? After what it had done to Bartram? He wished he could help, but, Christ, he didn't want to end up like that.

Rucker screamed. Barbs buried themselves in his ankles. They tore and burned. They held tighter. The pain shot through his being, and his only thought was that he wished they would rip his feet off so he didn't have to feel the torment any longer.

He rolled onto his back and aimed his Glock at the tentacles. He fired three shots. Each pierced a limb; none of them seemed to help. Three holes ripped through the strange black flesh, but it immediately sealed, then squeezed him tighter.

"Fuck!" Rucker screamed. Other tentacles hovered around the creature's center, waving like dancing snakes, as the ones that had him dragged him over the threshold into the house.

Karl winced, dreading what he knew was coming. It would be the same as what had happened to the other officer. The same as what had happened at the Mertzs. Or would it? He didn't want to go to jail, but he didn't want to see that same massacre happen to this guy. He surely didn't want those black arms to grab him and puree his body into the same god-awful mess.

A siren wailed in the distance. More police were coming. But they wouldn't be here soon enough to help Rucker. Probably not soon enough to see the real killer.

Karl was compelled; he had to do something. He ran past his garage and threw open the shed. On the right, beside the chainsaw and lawnmower, was the ax. He seized it and ran back to the front door.

Officer Rucker had tossed his firearm. He screamed without end–inhaling, exhaling; the sound was unrelenting. He held onto the door frame with everything he had as the oozing black arms yanked at him, stretched him in mid-air, pulling him toward their confluence.

Karl stopped short in the entryway. His eyes went wide as he saw the officer's legs, cut to the bone, skin and muscle nearly scraped clean on one and elongated on the other. He took a breath and raised the ax.

Rucker didn't even realize Karl had returned. His face was

a distorted expression of agony.

"Ah!" Karl swung.

The steel blade sliced through both tentacles, and an inhuman howl shook the home. Tentacles, the dismembered and the full, shot back into the black fog. A high-pitched scream flooded the house. The sound made Karl think his ears were bleeding.

He grabbed one of the officer's hands and dragged. He squeezed the man's hand so hard, he worried he might crack a bone but dared not pull any less. The tentacles could return. They could grab again at any second.

He dragged the policeman across the driveway and let go in the grass between the parking pad and the pasture. Officer Rucker moaned and pulled his legs into his hands.

The house shook. It seemed to cry like a toddler who didn't get its way. This wasn't the end.

Karl took a step toward his Jeep, then checked his pockets. He didn't bring his keys.

Which way to go? More police were coming. Karl had to get out of there. But he sensed the thing in the cloud was still inside. His keys were hanging just by the door, but should he risk going in? He had to. That, or go to jail for killing the neighbor and a cop–after the way they had come to his house and the death of Bartram, he was sure he'd get all the blame–no matter what Rucker had seen.

Karl darted to the door. He planned to reach around the doorframe and grab the keys without setting a foot inside. Then, he would turn and sprint back. It didn't happen that way.

As Karl reached the mat with a giant fall-colored *Hello*, he stopped in his tracks. The black cloud had swollen again. Six tentacles emerged from the racing torrent unlike the others.

They were larger, twice as thick as the previous ones. Instead of claws at their tips, these had what looked like mouths–fang-lined jaws that spread as they shot toward Karl.

"Shit!" Karl grabbed at the keys and felt only wall. His eyes were glued to the vision of death and pain racing toward him. He reached higher. He felt the dangling metal in his fingers and grabbed even higher. The keys filled his grip, and he closed his hand and ran.

Fangs snapped behind his heels. Their sharp clack chilled his bones. They sounded close, so close he didn't want to look, didn't want to know. He ran as hard as he could.

The sound of barking came from inside the house. It was deep and bellowed through the door. Karl didn't turn to see, but it sounded like the impossible. It sounded like Brady.

Karl grabbed the door to the old Jeep and flung it open. He leaped inside and slammed it. As he started the engine and threw the vehicle into reverse, Karl chanced a glance at what was behind him.

The tentacles were gone. The house shook, bathed in darkness. Through the door, Karl saw the fog bulge and converge on itself. He could swear it looked like it was fighting something.

Karl backed and turned. He regarded the officer one last time. Alive. Maybe that would be one thing in his favor. He sped down the driveway.

Chapter Three

The old Jeep rattled as it fought its way up the grade. Karl watched his rearview. Nothing coming after him. He watched the road ahead, and there they were, blue lights two hills away.

The strobes dimmed as the police raced down the hill opposite his, and Karl killed his headlights and turned onto the next dirt road. He drove a short way and stopped, put the Jeep in *Park*, killed the lights, and waited.

The cops tore down the road, their tires spitting gravel. The road was a fifty-five-mile zone, and they had to have been going ninety.

Karl gave the sirens a moment to fade. He rested his head on the wheel and his hands on his lap. That was when he felt it again. The large stone disc. It was in his pocket. How? The cop had taken it, dropped it on the floor in his living room. How was it in his pocket *again*?

Karl wrestled the thing free from his pocket and examined

it. The curves and crevices of its carvings shone in the rising moon's light. He still couldn't make any sense of the writing, but the shapes... They were familiar. They looked like the undulating currents of fog that rose and returned to that strange thing. He looked closer at the disc and swore he saw tentacles now.

"Those weren't there before." Karl got a chill. It was an October evening; he would have guessed it was around fifty degrees. It felt closer to thirty, and more and more, apprehension enveloped him.

A feeling settled inside his gut that there was no way out. It reminded him of being caught as a kid for stealing a Blowpop from the gas station. They'd called his mother, and he had to sit next to the register and wait. He had watched the customers come and pay and go, and he knew that each one was aware of what he had done. They knew he was bad. His mother was coming, and she would say he was bad. And there was nothing he could do. Punishment was coming. The word *reckoning* rang in his head. It vibrated in his mind the same way it had when he was arrested four years ago–when the cops found the bag of coke Sammy Rogers had left in his back seat. It wasn't Karl's fault it was there, but he had enough on his record that he would catch the reckoning. This wasn't Karl's fault either, but he'd done enough questionable shit in his life that he wished he hadn't–enough that something was eventually going to catch up to him. And that was it.

Karl shook his head. The reckoning was back. It had its claws in him. He didn't understand how or what it was, but this strange universal force was here for him now. It was going to use him and punish him and spit him out cold and shredded.

Karl's thoughts went to Amanda's face. Her sweet smile.

If he ran like he was expecting he'd have to, he wouldn't be able to see her again–not for a long while. His eyes welled with sadness thinking about it. He'd already spent three years without her, now this.

"Goddammit!" Karl pounded the steering wheel and tossed the disc out onto the gravel road. He threw the Jeep into *Drive* and took off.

Officer Mitchell Rucker waited in agonizing pain for what seemed like hours. His body trembled, and his breath grew shallow. It had been thirty minutes since the attack when the ambulance arrived, and the EMTs loaded him inside. On the way to Custer Falls Memorial Hospital, they wrapped his legs in bandages, started his IV, put an oxygen mask over his face, and reassured him that he was going to be okay. That, he thought, was one of the most oversized loads of bullshit he'd been fed in quite a while. At least one of his feet was going to have to be amputated; he was sure of that. He only hoped they'd be able to save the other.

His phone was in his pocket, and he debated calling Margery. They'd been divorced for eight months, and the wounds were still fresh, so he was slow to decide if he wanted her around. She would come if he called; he knew that. She'd come if anyone called. He wouldn't be able to stop that from happening at some point. The question was how soon did he feel like having her show up, and how upset was she going to be if he didn't call her right away?

Screw it, he thought. She could wait.

Rucker's head was getting lighter, and he wondered if it

was the morphine or whatever the hell they were giving him or if it was blood loss. He'd lost a lot. He was surprised he was still conscious after losing so much–but a lot that night had surprised him.

That had been the most grotesque crime scene he'd witnessed in his twenty-one years on the job. He couldn't fathom how it had been done. Then, there was the Chambers' house–it was clean, they had him, then out of nowhere–that cloud, the tentacles, the walls, ceiling, floor, covered with... His gut convulsed, and for a moment, he was worried he was going to puke inside the oxygen mask.

He settled himself, but the image of those tentacles around his leg refused to give way. The claws, the unearthly stench that oozed from them–he could still smell it creeping from under his bandages.

It was then that his mind began to drift. It was a different kind of weightlessness he felt though, not one of losing the world, but more the feeling of gaining another. It was a tingling warmth that crawled around inside his mind, and he couldn't fight the idea that it was coming from his wounds. Coming from the thing that had caused his wounds.

The mountains west of Custer Falls lay shrouded in the deepest hours of night when Karl arrived at Sean Murphy's cabin. Sean had been Karl's friend as far back as friends could be made. It ended, though, four years ago when Karl was sentenced to prison.

Karl was surprised how many relationships ended that day; how many of his *friends* chose not to believe him when he said honestly that the coke wasn't his. That he wasn't dealing that stuff. He wasn't the picture of sobriety by any sense of the word, but he had long been out of that game.

He tried to understand Sean's position. He was a deacon in his church with two little girls–one the same age as Amanda. Associating with a convicted felon, one charged with narcotics violations, was sure to ruffle feathers in his adult life. Karl didn't want to hold it against the man, but tonight, he looked at the loan of Sean's hunting cabin as a price he would collect for being wronged.

The lights were out; the generator off. It assured Karl no one was there. He thought for a moment about switching on the gennie and decided against it. There wouldn't be anyone close enough to hear it right now, but if some cop got the bright idea to look for him up here, the noise would give him away.

Karl drove past the cabin and parked the Jeep around back, on the other side of the woodshed. It wasn't perfect, but it would hide the vehicle at a glance.

Branches creaked from above. A layer of clouds had moved in and blocked the moon. Wind rushed past Karl's face, and he shivered. He wished he had been able to pack a few things before leaving home. A jacket, a flannel, even an extra shirt or two would have been nice.

The cabin door was locked. The key, however, was under the exact same oil drum on the side of the cabin as it had always been.

The inside was musty, the air thick with dust from at least a few years of disuse. Karl shone the flashlight from his phone and found the cots in the back. He was hungry and pretty sure Sean still had dehydrated food stored in the cabinets in the camp-style kitchen, but for now, he'd leave it. Maybe in the morning. Right now, he wanted the damn cuffs off his wrists.

In a bucket, by the sheet of plywood and sawhorses used as a table, Karl found Sean's tools. A hammer, a chisel, a pair of pliers; he hoped they would be enough.

Karl's mind drifted as he worked on his cuffs. He remembered this cabin filled with music, drinks, laughing, friends. He remembered similar occasions at his house, at other friends' houses. It weighed on him how few of those times he had these days. He generally tried not to let it bother him. He tried to be okay with having lost his friends, his wife, his social life. But now, with the bleakness of his future settling in, it tore at him. All over a stupid bag that wasn't even his.

He wished Brady were there. At least his dog. The one being who never judged him, always loved him, always loved being around him. And he was gone. His stomach ached. He ground his teeth and forced his eyes shut–made them seal, so hopefully tears wouldn't escape.

It took longer than he hoped, but Karl removed the cuffs and moved to the cots. The one he chose was as stiff as ever. It squealed as he lay on top of it. Karl didn't care. After an hour of driving through the mountains, his heart pounding, hoping to find safety, he'd found it. Or at least, he thought so.

Karl closed his eyes and patted down his body as he stretched. And there it was. In his pocket. The goddamn disc.

It was a dream. Karl knew it had to be. There was a surreal atmosphere that phased through his thoughts as only dreams do. There was a sense of dread, the impending doom of the start of a nightmare. There was also a truth that something important was coming, and despite the fear that mounted in his bones, he knew he had better pay attention.

Because it was also real. He knew that as well. A concreteness weighed heavily within the sensory input before him that he couldn't deny. The dampness of the air, its chill, the tightness of his boots on his feet. It told him to be careful.

The ground below Karl was red dirt. It was chunky, like clay that had been dug up and smoothed by hand, though not very well. A cloud of grayish-blue hung around him, restricting his view to only a few feet in any direction. And beside him sat Brady.

He didn't drop to his knees and praise the dog or greet him as if he hadn't seen him since the gunshot and untimely burial. Instead, he stood next to his companion as they always had because there was no sense of reuniting—there was a truth in Karl's mind that said they had never been separated.

The haze smelled like sulfur, and it began to itch Karl's nose. Something between a howl and a scream drifted over the obscure breeze. The call was returned from the other direction. Something dragged itself across the dirt beyond Karl's sight, and wetness dripped into the red earth as it moved.

The skin on Karl's arms and legs rose in goosebumps. His muscles tensed.

A hard wind blew, and the drifting haze was scattered into oblivion. In front of Karl was a valley loomed over by enormous, red mountains. Their rocky slopes seemed to move, but as Karl watched, he didn't see it happening. He knew they were changing in front of him, that the sharp peaks and narrow crevices were shifting and sliding, but his eyes couldn't find the proof. He heard rocks falling and rolling but saw nothing. And the eeriness chilled his blood.

The valley itself was slim yet full. Reddish-brown stone ruins dotted the terrain, hosting dead trees and barren bushes between them. The buildings radiated power, an old power that made the air buzz, even in its desolation.

Brady watched the landscape with suspicion. When Karl started walking toward the ruins, he growled and followed.

Dead bushes and grasses brushed against Karl's legs as he walked. They scratched at his clothes and boots, and Karl knew he was lucky they were dead. The world was sharp at every angle, rough on every surface, and if it could breathe, Karl knew it would eat him alive.

The closest of the ruins was a round-roofed temple with stone pillars and a vast open interior. It reminded him of the Jefferson Memorial in Washington, D.C., only in its center was not a beloved leader. There stood a ghastly statue of something Karl couldn't comprehend, and the more he tried, the more his head ached, the more the sharp edges of the world around him dug into his mind. Long stone tentacles stretched in every direction, barbed, mouthed, spiked, and some even with hands. Karl tried to see the center of the beast, to understand the thing that all these limbs extended from, but he couldn't. It seemed masked under its tendrils, under Karl's dream.

Karl wondered at the truth. Was something hiding the monster from him, or was he hiding it from himself? Was his brain protecting him from the image, knowing the reality might drive him mad?

Writing circled the statue, carved into the floor. Lines and lines of words in a language that Karl couldn't read. He circled the room, following the words, hoping for a glimpse or clue into the thing that seemed to be attached to him. He found one thing. An image of the disc and nothing else.

Rage flooded over Karl. Why was this happening? Why was he here? Why was this beast attached to *him*? He raced to the closest hanging tentacle, one whose end was shaped into a fanged mouth. He grabbed the statue's limb and yanked. He tried to rip it down and break it. He screamed at the monstrosity with everything his dream would allow.

The tentacle creaked. Flakes of stone crumbled to the floor. A line of spider-webbing cracks raced down the thing until stone fell away, and a black, oozing limb hissed in Karl's hands. Thorns stood from the tentacle, piercing Karl's fingers. A mouth-ended arm swung around and shot at Karl's gut. Its teeth dripped with black pus as they spread.

Karl could barely scream before the fangs sunk deep into his belly. The pain was hot and unreal. It was a stinging fire that encased his body and ripped into his limbs. He expected the thing to tear away the hunk of flesh it had in its mouth, but it didn't. It held still as if its job were merely to grab hold of him and make him suffer.

A voice spoke inside Karl's mind. Its words were whispers with stretched sibilance. "Stop fighting. You are ours now. There is no escape."

Karl pushed. He tried to back away, but the pain was too intense to move.

Brady growled and barked. He leaped and sunk his teeth into the snake-like thing. Black blood sprayed from the wound, drenching the dog's face and spilling onto the floor. It smelled putrid, reeking of earth and vomit.

Karl shot up in his bed with a gasp. He rubbed his stomach where the beast had bitten him. There was no wound, but tingling bumps ringed the spot. A circle of scars the size of the monster's fangs decorated his belly.

By the time morning came, four different doctors had examined Officer Rucker's legs. The first one had warned the officer to prepare for amputation. The second one wasn't so sure. When she removed the bandages to inspect the wound, it looked as though the torn muscle that had been stripped from his bone and stretched down to his ankles was moving back into place. The muscles seemed to be growing back into position.

The second doctor called the third. The third called the first back in, and together they all called the fourth. Each took a turn examining his calves and ankles, all saying they had never seen anything like it.

Rucker was so high on painkillers he paid little attention to the doctors. He'd already come to the conclusion that he would lose his feet, and accepting any of their nonsense claims of miraculous healing would only devastate him later. He didn't look down. He stared into the ceiling as the doctors talked and tried to block them out. Until he couldn't.

The meds in his system must have been wearing off because as the first rays of sunlight came through the window, an immense wave of pain rushed up Rucker's legs. He screamed and looked down, startling all four doctors.

The MDs clutched their clipboards and their phones.

Rucker stared in horror. His muscles were not moving into place or growing as those idiots had mumbled–at least not as they had said. His flesh around the wound had turned black. Black muscle, black bone, black ankles, black toes. The tissues that had been ripped away were rejoining themselves, but not in pink and red human flesh. No. The thing that was growing there was anything but human. It was black and slimy. Oozing, writhing, onyx meat filled the gap between his feet and his shins. And above his shins, the blackness was rising up his legs.

"Get it off me! Get it off!" Officer Rucker screamed. He grabbed at his legs and dug his fingers into the wound. Pain crashed through his system, but he didn't stop. He tore into the inhuman tissue and pulled it, ripped it.

"Stop!" a doctor shouted, followed by another. The third called for a nurse. The fourth and the first seized Rucker's hands as he rent back a string of black muscle and tendon that stretched from his shin to his heel.

"No!" Rucker shouted.

Three nurses burst into the room.

"Get it off!" He screamed. "Cut it off!"

Rucker yelled as much and as loudly as he could. He pleaded for them to listen. Why couldn't they see it? Why weren't they removing his feet? Cutting away the blackness? Were they blind?

He howled until a nurse plunged a syringe into his thigh, and the world drifted away.

CHAPTER FOUR

Karl had spent an hour trying to understand his dream until falling back asleep. The second time he awoke in the small cabin was to midmorning sunlight, a skull-splitting headache, and a feeling that he had slept for only half the night. On the bright side, there were no additional scars.

The cabin's "kitchen" held a single bank of cabinets and a gas-powered camp stove with an empty tank. In the cabinet, he found an unopened bag of beef jerky, a half-dozen cans of ravioli, and a box of dehydrated lasagna packages. The directions for the dehydrated stuff asked for hot water, of which he had none, so he opted for the canned pasta.

As he chewed the first bite of cold ravioli, he remembered why he hadn't touched the stuff since childhood. He decided that if the end of the world came and his rations were between dog food and this, he'd take the dog food.

He set the can aside and opened the jerky. His teeth sank

in and tore it apart. Not a perfect breakfast, but good enough.

As his mind woke up and he started to process the day before, Karl removed the disc from his pocket and set it on the floor in front of him. He seemed to remember tossing it through the cabin door at one point during the night, and here it was again. Again! Why was this thing attached to him?

Karl studied the engraving. The whirling circles now showed tentacles with fanged mouths and tentacles with human-like hands. Why was it changing?

He stared at it, watching it intently. Was it going to vanish and reappear in his pocket? After half a minute, it remained where he had placed it. He chewed on another chunk of jerky and pondered.

How long had that thing been under the china cabinet? Did his mother know it was there? He remembered the carvings on the side of the wood and examined the disc again. He felt there was something there. He remembered the writing in his dream, the symbols on the floor. Those, the wood carvings, the disc– they didn't say the same things, but all seemed to use the same alphabet. It occurred to Karl that the ring of words had encircled the statue in his dream. It only attacked him when he was inside the ring with it. The thing couldn't get out of the ring to get him. Words on the china cabinet had effectively circled the disc–until he moved it.

Chills ran over Karl's being. He had done this. The china on the table and the floor; that was a call, an outburst, a ploy to get him to look inside and remove the disc. He had been used to set this thing free. And now, it was his job to put it back.

When Officer Rucker awoke, his legs ached. His skull was pounding. He tried to rub his head but found himself in restraints. The leather bands held his hands near the bed rail. He pulled and wriggled against the leather, but they were stubborn, unyielding.

Rucker looked down to his feet. They were shrouded by his sheet, but he saw darkness through the sheer white fabric. Was it a blanket? A dark bandage? An image came to him of the dark, oozing flesh that had tried to grow on his legs.

"No, no, no," Rucker chanted and kicked at his covers.

The sheet lifted and fell, granting him only a glimpse into the darkness of his lower half. He kicked again. The sheet billowed upward and floated down. During the window of vision, what Rucker saw made his heart jump. The shock rippled down his body. From his toes to the edge of his hospital gown–he was black. Onyx, shimmering with inhuman ooze. The sheet came back down, resting on his feet. He pulled them back and laid them on top of the white bedding.

Rucker's heart pounded. His chest tightened. He watched the skin on his lower half and saw patterns undulate below the surface. Something was inside his flesh–not just changing its color–something was inside him and moving. He pictured worms digging their way through soil, then realized: tentacles. Something's tentacles were inside his body and shifting, sliding, traveling, and–changing him?

He looked at the edge of his gown. He wondered how far up his body the slimy new flesh had crawled. He shuddered at the thought of his genitals. Were they transformed as well? Was his prick now a tentacle as well? Was the encroaching entity close to his heart?

Sweat ran down Rucker's temple. He realized he was

pulling on his restraints so hard, his hands were growing numb. *What do I do?* he wondered. He wanted to scream for help but remembered the last time. They didn't see it. They had thought he was crazy and knocked him out. He needed to get out of this bed, out of this place, and find someone that would believe him–help him.

Rucker felt a lightness take hold of his thoughts. He didn't understand it, but his nervousness was fading and his anger rising. He gazed into the wall beyond his bed and began to see through it. Not into the next room but into another place. He saw decrepit buildings, ruins that were once temples, but now served as graves. He saw a swirl of black smoke and fog and remembered the Chambers' house, the tentacles. But this time, there were no tentacles, nothing trying to grab him and possibly eat him or rip him to shreds. What he saw instead was a being with a power that seeped inside his bones. It was power that called on him. It praised him and soothed him. It made him want to be with it. He wanted to serve it. He would be honored to serve; he needed to serve.

Black tissue emerged from Rucker's sleeve. It spread down his arm. It passed his bicep and covered his elbow. He felt its slick slime easing him, cooling him, calming him. It moved up his neck and onto his chin.

"You will serve us," a slow booming voice said. Its Ss trailed like the hiss of a snake. It was beyond the wall, inside the vision, but also inside Rucker's mind. There was an accent attached to its words, but not one he had ever heard. It sounded alien to his world.

"Yes," was all Rucker could say. "I want to..."

"Find the one with our amulet. He has betrayed us. Kill him."

Rucker's mind was rushed with visions of last night, Karl Chambers. He needed to kill Karl Chambers. "Yes."

"Now. Before he returns it. Before he imprisons us again."

"Yes."

Rucker blinked, and the wall was once again only a wall. His skin, his body, however, continued to change. The black oozing tissue stretched under his leather bonds and enveloped his hands. It encircled his face and consumed it in otherworldly flesh. Blackness covered Rucker's eyes, and when he opened them again, the world was not the same.

The walls in his hospital room melted away, reflecting waves of false reality. They dripped with the condensation of false belief. Rucker now saw that the life he had been living for nearly forty-five years had been a ruinous lie. He had been adhering to the foolish assumptions of tiny minds about everything. The world they considered physical; it was no more than a container of filth, designed to hold his kind so that they might worship and feed those higher than themselves. It was a farm and a feeding pit, and the structures that he and his fellow humans had believed were the laws of physics were mere playthings to the being he served. It was as though the world were made of strings, and he could now see the thread, the patterns, and the beings holding it all. They were all asleep–waiting–but he would do his job and rectify that.

Rucker looked at his hands. The blackened meat looked so silly, strapped inside the cured strips of cowhide. His thumbs and fingers shrunk and liquefied, slurped up into the elongating flesh that was once his palm. The appendages became pointed, sharply tipped tentacles, and slid free of their bonds.

The machines beside the bed beeped, and Rucker turned to the right. His legs hung from the mattress, floppy, slimy tentacles. Their tips waved and slid across the space, no longer attached to feet. A dozen barbed spikes extruded through the blackened skin, and he stepped down from the bed.

A nurse in blue scrubs opened the door and rushed into the room. "Mr. Rucker?" Her eyes were full of questions, but she was not as shocked as Rucker had expected. "You need to get back in bed."

Behind the nurse, Margery stepped in. Her face was long, her eyes wet. She brought with her the scent of cigarette smoke, though she had quit three years ago. "Mitchell?"

Did they not see him? See what he had become? His entire body, his entire life, had been transformed into a divine entity, blessed by the one he now served, and they acted as though he were still nothing but a feeble human. They were as blind to it as the rest of them were blind to the world right in front of them.

"Sir?" the nurse asked.

Rucker lifted his right arm. It stretched across the room and buried barbs into the nurse's neck. He flicked his tentacle, and it unwound from her, peeling away the skin on her throat and ripping her arteries open.

Blood sprayed on Margery in two lines that striped her face like a human candy cane. She opened her mouth to scream, and Rucker's tentacle darted down her throat.

The nurse didn't speak. She gurgled. Her fingers clutched at her neck for the skin that now hung from Rucker's right tentacle. She slipped to her knees.

Rucker's flesh, without direction, absorbed the skin, fat, and blood on its barbs. His arms and legs sprouted dozens of smaller tendrils that reached and wrapped around the nurse. They sucked and slurped at her body while the one inside his ex-wife spread and began eating her from the inside.

Rucker watched with wide eyes. He felt his insides strengthen, his lust grow. When each tiny tentacle returned to his flesh and soaked back into his skin, not even a pair of slime-covered bone piles remained on the floor.

He inhaled. It was a meaningless thing, an act of a mortal. He felt his flesh's disregard of the useless gases, and he moved on to the door.

Without much hope of it working, Karl tried his phone. No signal. The cabin was too remote.

He wanted to check the news, to see if what happened at home was being reported, and to hopefully get an idea whether or not police would be waiting at his door. He wondered if he drove down the mountain and got close to the main road if he would have enough signal to use the Internet.

Something about this idea sparked a memory. Today was Saturday. Today was the day his ex-wife Suzanne would be coming back into town and dropping Amanda off around seven. If she hadn't heard the news, that is.

Karl panicked. What would happen if they heard the news that he was wanted for the murder of his neighbors and two officers? What would Amanda think of him? What would happen if they didn't hear and showed up at his house? They could run into police and crime scene tape. And what if that thing came back?

Chills rushed over Karl. His heart raced. The image of Bartram made him nauseous, him being dragged into that swirling vortex of smoke and spit back out. Thinking of Amanda going anywhere near something like that made his hands shake.

He needed to go. First, to the road to see if his phone had a signal, then to the house to stop Suzanne and Amanda from going inside.

He wasn't sure how the thing worked, if it could show up without him being there or if it were following him around, but either way, he couldn't take the chance.

Karl rushed from the cabin and jumped into his Jeep. He put his key into the ignition and began to feel lightheaded. Something was wrong. He put his hands on his temples and rubbed. They dropped to his lap, resting on top of the hard circular outline of the disc in his pocket, and then he passed out.

Officer Rucker took a cab to his home, ignoring the questions from the driver about his lack of clothing. When asked if he at least had a wallet to pay with, Rucker told the cabby to shut the fuck up and drive.

The taxi stopped in front of the garage door, and the driver held his palm out to Rucker. "Twenty-three fifty. And I hope your cash isn't hidden too far under that smock."

Rucker looked into the driver. He had started to see more than just the strings that pulled on the world, but the power behind it. He saw within the cabby, inside the center of his skull, a glowing orb of light. If Rucker had to guess, he would have ventured it was the man's soul. He didn't care what it was, though. What he cared about was that it looked delicious. He had been nearly salivating the last mile of the trip and holding himself back to make sure he made it to his house.

Rucker glanced outside the vehicle. He lived on a decent

acre-sized parcel, so he had some privacy, but Mrs. Millweather across the street still liked to lookie-loo and gossip with the rest of the old-timers in the subdivision. Her car was not in her driveway. *Good enough.*

Rucker felt his leg tentacles split. They divided into a dozen smaller tendrils and stretched under the driver's seat. The officer leaned forward onto the passenger seat and looked into the driver's eyes.

The cabby twitched. His gaze darted forward and back to Rucker. The vehicle's air had gone cold and that primal survival instinct was starting to nag at the driver. It said he should be getting out of this situation–quickly–and the hairs on his arms raised.

"You know what?" the cabby said. His voice was light, trembling. "You said you're a cop–how about we make this one on the house?" He nodded nervously. His hands balled into fists around the steering wheel. His mouth had gone dry, and now it clicked as his jaw moved.

Rucker's tentacles loosely encircled the cabby's feet and walked up the insides of his jeans. As they reached the man's knees, Rucker smiled. It was an unintentional movement, a reaction to anticipation, as though a waiter had set the perfect looking ribeye in front of him; the scent of seared outer edges, the salty sense of seasoning and butter, and the pooling of blood below. His mouth began to water.

The cabby bore a confused expression and cracked a nervous smile in response.

Rucker raised his hand. His fingers split into five black, clawed tendrils. They shot toward the driver's head and swarmed around the top of his skull. The man opened his mouth, but before he could scream, before blood could slip between the claw's razer tips and the cabby's scalp, Rucker's lower limbs seized the man tightly. Officer Rucker's mouth spread, revealing five rows of fangs, and they closed onto the cabby's face.

When Karl opened his eyes, he was no longer in the Jeep. He lay on the ground beside the vehicle, pine needles and dirt in his hair. His head ached, and despite just waking up, he was exhausted. Had he fallen out?

The disc was in his hand. He didn't notice at first, not until he looked. His palm, his fingers, his arm were numb. Cold. But there was no blood this time. Had the creature come? Or had something different happened?

It occurred to Karl, a subconscious thought that bloomed into a realization, an image that became a strain of logic: He saw a battery. *He* was the battery. This thing in his hand–it was feeding on him. It was using him somehow to do its bidding, appear and make its kills. But since it didn't appear, didn't kill this time, what was it doing with the fuel it took from him?

He tossed the disc into the brush, knowing it would only be a matter of time before it reappeared in his pocket. He looked at the sky and wondered how long he'd been lying there. His phone read 4:43 p.m., and home was two hours back through the mountains. If he were going to make it there by seven for Amanda and Suzanne, he needed to hurry. He stood, and the numbness began to fade from his hand.

"Gotta get home."

Chapter Five

When Officer Mitchell Rucker returned to Karl Chambers' home, he was dressed in his uniform and driving his state-issued cruiser. As he expected, the CSI team had gone through the place and left. So had the detectives. All that remained now was a single county deputy who had been asked to keep an eye out for Chambers' return and shoo away any reporters who showed up.

The county brass expected the story to reach the national news in the next twenty-four hours, which would mean more bad press for the area. Custer Falls had been through enough bad press over the past few years to last a lifetime–some had even started calling it the murder capital of the Northwest. Of course, that couldn't be true with the limited size of the population, but there had been enough gruesomeness to merit the comparison, the rash of killings in the '90s alone would warrant that.

Rucker parked beside the county cruiser as rain began to fall. He rolled down his window, and the deputy did the same.

"Looks like the fun's over," Rucker said.

"Yeah, they're all done." The deputy wore a brown mustache with a badge and a nameplate above it that read *Matthews*.

"So, you're on babysitting detail?" Rucker could feel his new flesh oozing, crawling under his clothes, soaking the fabric in black fluids. He was still amazed that no one else could see it.

"Yup. I'm here 'til shift change. Just sitting."

Rucker watched the glow in the man's head wobble as he talked. It fluttered and shifted like a flame in the wind from golden to orange to pinkish. He wondered what this one would taste like. The cabby had been delicious, better than any food or drink or drug he'd had in his previous life. It was warm and savory with just a slightly sweet aftertaste. He wondered if they were all as good. Or were some better? He wondered if anyone would miss the deputy in the next few hours–but he may get calls on his radio. Rucker decided it wasn't worth the risk–not until he'd dealt with Karl Chambers.

"Well, I'm going to be here for a bit," Rucker said.

"Yeah?"

"Have to gather some info for my report. Maybe take a few minutes to say a word or two to Bartram."

The deputy nodded. "It's unlocked."

"Thanks." Rucker tried for an honest, convincing smile. "You know, if you want to take lunch, run any errands or anything–I'll be here to watch the place. I imagine staring at this shithole for another five hours would be a pain in the ass, so if you want to take off..."

The deputy contemplated. "How long will you be here?"

"Two-three hours. At least until eight-thirty or nine."

"You won't take off early?"

"Not if you aren't back. I won't get you in a jam." *Whatever it takes*, Rucker thought. *Now get out of here.*

The deputy nodded again. "I'll take you up on that. Grab some grub and–maybe something else." He smirked at Rucker.

Rucker smirked back as the deputy started his cruiser.

After a final glance, the county officer headed down the driveway, and Mitchell Rucker stood from his vehicle. He walked to the trunk, removed an ax, and headed inside.

Karl had been pushing the old Jeep up and down winding hills, around sharp switchbacks, and over rocky dirt roads. He'd been pushing it too hard, and the engine started overheating.

He didn't usually have much trouble with the vehicle, but he didn't usually drive like this. He babied it. Now, as he reached the main road, right where he'd be within sight of passing motorists who might recognize him, the temperature gauge hovered a hair below red. He could feel the heat coming through the firewall from the engine compartment. He didn't want to, but he'd have to stop and let the thing cool if he didn't want it to break down.

The day was moving on toward dusk. The overcast sky had faded from gray to orangish pink, and raindrops were patting against the windshield. He sat with the vehicle turned off and twitched. His foot hopped. His fingers tapped at the wheel. His mind raced with angst, worry, and fear that couldn't be subdued. It soaked his skin and tingled. His jaw ached from grinding his teeth together.

It was a little after six, and he had thirty minutes left to drive until he was home. That was cutting it too close. He wanted to get there and put this damn disc back where it belonged. Because God help him if he still had it in his pocket and Amanda and Suzanne showed up. If they showed up.

He'd checked the local news sites, and there he was on the home pages of both. "Suspected Cop Killer Loose," one website said. "Manhunt!" the other screamed.

He tried calling Suzanne a dozen times, and each time the call went straight to voicemail. He wasn't a techie and wasn't sure, but he thought that meant she was in a dead zone. He thought about leaving messages but didn't. What if the cops got a hold of them somehow? He'd keep trying instead.

He dreaded not knowing what would happen next. What would happen if the thing appeared at his house and Suzanne and Amanda were there? Would he pass out like he did at the Mertzs' house? Would he freeze and have to watch his daughter and ex-wife ripped to shreds? No. He couldn't let that happen. He had to get there early. The damn disc had to go back.

Karl started the Jeep. The temperature was lower, around three-quarters toward red. It would have to do.

Suzanne barreled down I90 in her '01 Honda Accord and just knew she would be late dropping off Amanda. Not that it bothered her that much. Her evening plans after the drop-off were to spend the night drinking whiskey and fucking Brad Lavar while the kid was happily at the ex's house–but she really didn't want to hear Karl bitch about the time. She would have called him to let him know she was running late, and the bitching would probably have been less exhaustive. Unfortunately, her drunk-ass dropped her phone last night while dancing with Dan Avery, one of her high school crushes, and some asshole had stepped on it. He cracked the screen and the rest of the thing nearly in two. She figured that's what she got for buying a Walmart phone. But at least it saved her the hassle of adding Dan's number to her contacts after he only lasted thirty seconds in the lady's room stall.

Amanda flipped through her mother's book of '90s CDs, praying for the current album to finish so she could pick something else. It was her turn next if Suzanne kept her word, which she often didn't.

Seal finally stopped bellowing, the music faded, and Amanda had never been so happy to hit eject. She slipped in the next disc before her mother could ask what it was and began grinning at the Caribbean rhythm and piano as *Spice Up Your Life* began.

"No, no, no," Suzanne said, reaching for the radio. "No Spice Girls."

"*Mom!* You had your pick."

Suzanne relented and put her hand back on the wheel. She rolled her eyes and imagined getting home and guzzling a shot of Wild Turkey.

Amanda began chanting, "La la la la," in time with the music, and the miles passed.

They exited in Butte and took Highway 89 north. As soon as Amanda saw the sign, "Custer Falls 50 Miles," a shiver shook her entire body. Her thoughts went to her dad, and she got the feeling that something was wrong.

"You talk to Dad?" Amanda asked. Her face was tense, doubtful.

"You know my phone broke, hun. Last time we talked, we said seven o'clock, and I think we're going to make that." Amanda looked at the clock in the center of the dash. 6:05. She wanted to get there and hoped Dad was okay, but at the same time, the feeling that something was wrong made her want to drive the other way. Made her want to tell her mother to turn around and not look back. But that wasn't right.

She bit her lip, failing to notice her song had ended. Rain splatted against the windshield, and the sky darkened.

"My turn now," Suzanne sang. "Find me that Aerosmith's Greatest Hits CD–I think it's red."

Amanda fought the growing worry and flipped the pages.

Karl tried calling Suzanne's phone again. Straight to voicemail. He debated between a dead zone and her ignoring his calls. Had the cops talked to her yet? If she hadn't been out of town for a high school reunion, he'd be sure they did, but with her traveling, he didn't know what to think.

But what if they did get in touch with her? She would have told them he was supposed to meet her at his house at seven. They could have the SWAT team waiting for him to show up. He didn't know if Custer Falls even had a SWAT team, but with two state troopers in the mix, they'd be bound to do whatever it took to get him.

He glanced at his phone, and all the cop shows he'd ever seen ran through his mind. Could they track him? He'd heard kooks on Facebook say they could, seen it in movies, but was that real? He didn't know but figured he shouldn't take the risk. He powered it off and tossed it from the window.

The roads were lonely. The October air had chilled along with the engine, and Karl could feel the cold from the windshield even through the warmth of the Jeep's raging defrost. The wipers clunked as they shifted from left to right and right to left, and each *clunk* seemed like an impact on Karl's confidence. Could he pull this off? Get home and meet Amanda? Keep her safe from this monster? With each passing mile, his doubts grew.

He was almost there, only a few streets away when it occurred to Karl that he probably shouldn't go up his own road. It was a narrow, winding path through the woods at the mid-point, and that was a good place to get trapped. No, he should go another way.

He turned at the street just before his own, Red Spruce Lane. The end of the road joined a path where an old railway line once ran and connected that street to his own. It had been grandfathered in as a public easement once the tracks were removed, and his neighbors used it to cross back and forth without going down to the main road.

Raindrops smacked the Jeep, thumping against its steel skin like Karl hadn't heard in years. It was starting to look like the storms he'd seen in the tropics when he'd gone on vacation–nothing like the light dustings of precipitation that usually fall in Montana. He could barely discern his neighbors' homes through the downpour, and he was thankful. It meant they couldn't see him.

Karl reached the top of the hill and turned onto the easement. He drove halfway down and stopped where the trees parted and he could see his own driveway. He expected to see police cars, even a van of State Troopers ready to get their revenge on the asshole that had killed one of their own and wounded another. But there weren't any vehicles at all. The parking pad, the driveway, his street: They were all empty.

Some of the weight lifted from Karl's shoulders–not all of it, but more than he realized was there. He crept forward and turned onto his road, then slowly up his driveway. His eyes scanned the street. Nothing. The sides of his home. Nothing. He watched the windows in case they were hiding inside and waiting to spring on him. Nothing. Could he really be this lucky?

Karl parked and rushed toward the front door. Just because he was alone didn't mean it would stay that way. He envisioned police swarming up his driveway and stopping him before he could return the disc to its resting place. He imagined Suzanne and Amanda showing up just to be greeted by a swirling black fog and arms of death. This had to end–now.

The engine sputtered to stop, and as Karl climbed out of the Jeep, he felt the hard talisman in his pocket. He took a step toward the house, and a chill washed over him. Under the downpour, his flesh stood in goosebumps. His teeth went numb, and his stomach turned. He continued on with a gulp that clicked in his throat.

The doorknob was cold. It seemed to vibrate in a high key as Karl gripped and turned. And under the squeak of the widening door, Karl thought he heard a growl.

Chapter Six

From across the home, Karl heard the chime of his mother's grandfather clock. The gray sky faintly lit the living room. It would have been a good day to have a fire in the fireplace, a good day to sit cozily with Amanda on the couch and watch some bad movies. On any other weekend where blood and viscera didn't coat the walls, the ceiling, and the furniture, those things would have been nice.

Karl hurried through the living room, his gaze following the dried remains of Officer Bartram and into the dining room. He froze in place as his eyes met the blank spot on the wall where his mother's china cabinet was supposed to stand. His heart leaped into his throat.

The dining room table was on its side, tossed nearly into the kitchen. In its place were chunks of old-growth oak stained the color of the missing china cabinet. Splinters and hunks of wood carpeted the room, some intricate ruins and expertly crafted woodwork, some no larger or more identifiable than debris from a wood chipper.

"My God," Karl muttered. His hopes sank. That sense of dread spread from the stone bulge in his pants' pocket across his thighs and up into his belly. He wanted to puke. He pictured Amanda walking into his home at any moment, her face at the sight of the room's horror, overlaid with his own entrails, and a whirling angry cloud of tentacles moving toward her. His fingers shook.

What could have happened here? His thoughts went to the police–they wouldn't do this. The CSI guys? They may have looked inside or dismantled it with tools, but not this. This was barbarism, rage. He looked around the rest of the room and in the kitchen. An ax lay on the counter, and a pair of eyes gleamed back at him.

Karl took half a step backward. His flesh crawled with disgust. He watched the being in the kitchen move. It seemed to float around the counter and toward the dining room. Its shape was difficult to discern in the gloom of the dying afternoon light, but Karl watched as it rose and fell and seemed to swim inside itself. Its black pieces were like a hovering mound of faceless snakes. Oily, oozing skin slid across its surface and slurped as tentacles spread and reunited.

The mass of tendrils parted below the eyes, and a voice spoke. "Give me the amulet."

It was thin, almost whispering, but Karl knew it–and it wasn't the thing from his dream. It was the cop.

Karl took another step backward. His first thought was: *Fuck.* His second was: *Okay, give him the thing.*

The options raced through his head. He could be free of the stone. But what would happen after that? Would the once-cop thing take it and go? He didn't think so. Something told him that once the abomination in front of him had what it wanted, it would tear him to shreds. He watched the undulating arms hang with barbed thorns and gleaming claws. There was no way this thing would let him live. And what would it do next? What about when Amanda arrived? What if he were dead and in pieces and she walked through the door.

Karl clenched his fists and stepped back again. "No." The cabinet was destroyed, but there had to be another way to end this.

Tentacles grew from the hovering mass and slowly snaked their way across the floor toward Karl.

"Yessss," Rucker hissed.

Trails of black slime marked the floor. Karl watched each spine, barb, and claw move closer. A shot of panic tore through his system, wrenching his body around and sending him sprinting toward the front door.

Wood squeaked under his boots. His chest pounded. He grabbed the door jamb and swung himself outward as the toe of his left boot caught on the threshold.

Karl plummeted down, and all he could think of was each black thing racing at him. They would reach him. They would wrap around him and tear his flesh from his bone. They would drag him and rip him apart and take the stone.

His fingers touched the gritty concrete of his porch, bracing his fall, and a car engine reversed down his driveway.

Amanda shut the door to the Honda as Mom cranked up the radio. Mom looked back and reversed, and all Amanda could think was, *please don't drive after you get drunk tonight.* She was past worrying about her mother getting pregnant from any of her boyfriends; she'd heard Mom and Betty Hughes a year ago talking about how Mom had her tubes tied. A quick Google, and her hopes that one day she might have a little sister were swept away, never to be heard from again.

She carried her backpack toward Dad's front door, wiping rain from her brow. Dad rushed out, tripped, and slammed into the front porch.

"Dad!" Amanda ran toward the house.

Dad stared across the sidewalk with wide blazing eyes. His face was pale, and the cords on his neck stood up.

She froze. He stumbled forward and climbed to his feet. He moved toward her, outstretching his red, skinned palms.

"Go!" Dad screamed. He seized Amanda's arm and dragged her up the driveway. "We have to go. Into the Jeep."

"Dad?" She followed along, dragging her feet, nearly tumbling onto the asphalt. "What's–"

"Gotta go!" He flung the driver's door open. His eyes shot to the front of the house. His jaw clenched.

Through the front door, a tall, middle-aged state trooper walked. His hands rested on his belt, and his eyes were fixed on Dad.

"Get in!" Dad shouted.

Mom was gone. She drove onto the road and sped away. The Jeep's front tire exploded, followed by the rear.

Karl leaned in and hoisted Amanda in his arms. He leaped over the tentacle pinched between the rear tire's blown rubber and carried his baby girl across the parking pad and into the grass.

"Dad?" She shouted.

He squeezed her tight. If she squirmed, and he dropped her–only bad could happen then. He had to hold on, to keep her safe.

Rain wet his face and drenched his clothes. Wind blew past, numbing his nose and ears as the fall temperatures dropped and the sky turned ever darker. The grass squeaked softly underfoot, and Karl pivoted left, circling around to the back of his garage.

"Dad!" Amanda screamed. Her face was hard, tense.

"We have to move!" He screamed back. "He'll kill us."

Her eyes went in search of the officer. Her lips pursed.

Ten feet, and Karl set Amanda down over the dog run's chain-link fence. He leaped over and took her hand, running yet again. They reached the back door and darted inside.

Karl slammed the door and locked it. The home's interior was darkening by the second, hard to see, and the overwhelming stench of putrefying remains hit him yet again.

Amanda gaged. Her eyes traced the lines of Officer Bartram's entrails across the ceiling, and her mouth quivered. "D-d-d-d-d," she stuttered.

"Shit." Karl dragged her across the kitchen and into the master bedroom.

Pounding on the back door. *Crack*.

Karl slammed the bedroom door and locked it. It was a cheap, hollow-core door, installed during his mother's last renovation, and he knew it wouldn't stand up to anything. But he only needed a minute.

He pushed Amanda toward the bathroom. "Go in there. Lock the door. Don't open it unless I say."

"Daddy..." She whimpered.

"Go," He pushed her again.

She backed down the hallway.

Karl raced to the master closet. In the back, he spun the wheel of his gun safe's lock. *38.* His once stepfather had kept a dozen rifles in the six-foot-tall steel box. *12.* Karl's collection was much more meager, but if he could get to it... *27.*

Bang, bang, crack. The bedroom door caved in.

Karl pressed down on the handle. It clicked, but it didn't move. *Shit!* Had he entered the combination wrong?

Panic swept through his flesh. His heart pounded. His fingers were cold, and his breath trembling.

He spun the knob again. *38.*

Amanda. She was just in the bathroom, behind another cheap, shitty door. That asshole cop could get in there–get her so easily.

He spun it the other way. Around. *12.*

"Karl?" the cop said. "Let me see you, Karl."

He spun it back. *27.*

"Give me the amulet, Karl."

Through the sound of his own heavy breathing, Karl heard the slither of snakes across his bedroom floor. He pressed down on the handle. *Click.*

His heart jolted. The safe door swung open. Karl saw his savior, his 12 gauge tactical Mossberg. He seized it with unsteady hands, threw the strap over his shoulder, then pumped it. He swung around and aimed through his closet door. His heart jolted again.

Amanda stood in front of the six-foot-tall mass of draping tentacles. Her eyes were spread and fixed on Karl. A single black tendril hung loosely around her neck, another around her waist.

"Daddy?"

"Give me the amulet," Rucker said.

Karl's world raced through his mind. Amanda's smile as an infant. The giggle she made when Brady licked Cheeto dust from her fingers. The warmth when she wrapped her arms around him and hugged.

Karl imagined taking the shot. He could nail the thing's head with ease. But would a pellet strike Amanda? Would that thing be dead with one hit? Or would it have time to tighten its grip on her throat?

And what if he gave it the stone? There's no way it would just walk away and leave them. Was there? No, it would kill them anyway.

Karl felt the rain drip from his hair and run down his face. He felt the stiffness of the shotgun's stock against his shoulder. He smelled the scent of past gunsmoke on the weapon's blue steel.

What was he going to do?

"Daddy?" Amanda said. Tears streamed down her face, bulldozing through the drops of rain on her cheeks, her chin.

"The amulet," Rucker said.

Thunder cracked outside, and the sound of growling came down from the ceiling. It seemed to circle the room until it settled in front of Karl.

Karl glanced down. At first, he saw nothing, then the faint glow of something. An apparition. A shape familiar and welcome. It was a translucent form that looked like Brady.

The half lab, half hound, half shepherd of some kind, stood with legs tensed and body tight. He stared into the mass of swinging limbs with semi-parted lips and widening jaws. His growl grew louder.

"What is–" Rucker said.

Brady launched from the floor. He sprang like nothing Karl had ever seen. He was a blur in the room's dim light, one moment sitting, the next his face, his fangs, deep inside the mass of tentacles.

"No!" Rucker shouted.

Karl raised the shotgun. He aimed two inches above the top of the beast and squeezed the trigger.

Amanda screamed.

The shotgun fell from his hands and hung from his shoulder.

Tentacles and black ooze erupted across the room. A bubble of black gunk seemed to pop where the monster's head should have been, painting the ceiling, bed, and Amanda in a viscous slime.

The body of Officer Rucker collapsed under Brady's ghostly image, and Amanda fell beside it.

"Aman–" Karl lunged forward after his daughter. Her hands gripped the arm on her throat as blood leaked from beneath it. "I'm coming."

She gasped and pulled. More blood flowed. Karl grabbed the slimy thing around her neck. It was attached to her skin; its barbs inside her flesh.

Karl remembered hunks of meat torn from Bartram's body as the other monster ripped them free. "Wait," He told her. "Don't pull."

He leaped to his feet and darted to his dresser. From the top drawer, he grabbed his hunting knife and brought it over. He felt along the tentacle. It was tight, flexed, as if holding onto Amanda's throat was its only purpose.

Karl sliced into the tendril's meat, and black blood sprayed.

He carved deeper and deeper. The creature writhed and howled even louder. Karl sawed and dug until the limb fell free from the monster, limp, hanging only from his daughter.

"Amanda." He spun to see her face. Her eyes were open, her lips blue; she stared at the ceiling. She was dead.

Karl turned to stone. Cold seized him, standing every hair on end. "No," he muttered.

This couldn't be. She couldn't die. He killed the thing that was attacking her. He tore its arm free. It couldn't be too late. It was only a moment that he was away. Only a moment while he cut the tentacle loose. He stared into her eyes, the eyes of the only thing left on the Earth that he loved, and he burst into tears.

"No!" He pushed on her chest. He breathed into her mouth. Again and again, he breathed. He pushed. "Come back!" His eyes blazed red. He pushed. He breathed. But her heart remained still. Her lungs refused to move on their own. His eyes cried so hard he swore it was blood. His body convulsed and wanted to vomit. His gut clenched with wails.

Brady pulled his face from the mass of tentacles and joined Karl. He sniffed Amanda. He sniffed at the limb around her neck as it sizzled and melted away with the rest of them. A ghostly whimper left his lips, and he placed his head against her chest.

Amanda's eyes shot wide, and she belted a terrified scream.

Karl couldn't breathe. He smiled through rain and tears. He lunged and embraced her, pulled her from the floor and into his chest. Was this really happening? She was back? He loosened his grip enough to see her face and see that she was, in fact, alive, then sealed his arms around her yet again.

"Dad?" she moaned.

Brady looked at Amanda as if judging his work well done. Then, he bent down and growled at the stone in Karl's pocket, and Karl's leg began to go numb.

"No, no, no." Karl loosened and glanced at his pants. "Not now."

The small amount of light within the room drained to a bland, dying illumination. The color of the world faded. Wind blew across the back of Karl's head, and the rushing sound of that thing rose behind him.

Amanda in his arms, Karl jumped to his feet and darted past his bathroom, through the bedroom door, and into the kitchen.

The rushing sound of the beast came from behind him. It was the sound of hate, of anger, and it wanted him. It wanted to mete out its vengeance on him. Somehow it knew what he was up to. It knew he was going to imprison it back in that case, and it had sent Rucker there to stop him–to kill him. Now, that tentacled beast was going to do it itself.

Karl could feel it moving closer. Feel its tentacles stretching and crawling through his home. It was like he was connected to it, maybe through the disc.

He paused in the dining room and set down Amanda. "Go outside. Wait for me in the Jeep."

"Dad?" She stared back at him with wet, bulging eyes. "What's happening?"

"No time. Please go."

Tears streaked her face. "Daddy?"

He grabbed her and pulled her to his chest. He knew it might be the last time he could do this, and he felt himself sharing every inch of love he had within him. He felt the warmness between them, and he felt her trembling woes.

"I know you're scared, baby girl. I am too. But you have to go. Another bad thing is coming, and I need you out of here–safe. Please listen to me, and go."

She took a step back. Her lower lip curled in.

"Go, please. I can't protect you in here."

She backed further.

The ground shook. Wind raced through the kitchen.

"I love you." He shooed her back and wiped the tears from his eyes.

"I love you." She turned and ran for the door.

Karl stared at the shreds of oak piled over his floor. It was mixed with broken china, glass, and hardware.

He had to find a way to stop the thing. He couldn't run from the disc. Every time he tried, it showed up in his pocket. He had to get it back into its trap, seal it once again. It was the only way for him to get out of this situation.

Karl dug through the splinters and chunks, pieces of broken board and broken dish. He spotted a board with a symbol. It was from the right side of the cabinet. He kept digging and found another. He found a third, but it was broken into two pieces. Would that work? He didn't know, but he put the pieces into a pile and kept digging. There were at least two other symbols.

He set his hand on another piece, and a snap cracked the air above Karl's head. He saw a flash of black shoot by his face, and fear raced through his veins. He knew what would come next if it grabbed him.

"Shit!" He rolled to his left, and two tentacles slid past. Another tentacle went for his leg, and Karl moved again. It slid over his leg and split his jeans. Another, and he continued his dance. It sliced his other leg, and blood ran down his calf.

Karl seized the pile of boards he'd collected and ran toward the door.

The walls shook. The room, the view through the windows, the world, all seemed to be a blurring vision of black and white. His mind sank as he felt it drain him through the disc, but he refused to stop.

The floor vibrated below Karl's feet. He wanted to know how far he'd run, if he'd put any distance between himself and the thing, but he didn't dare turn back. He pumped his legs as hard as he could and felt a sting on the side of his face. He ducked through the front door and heard Brady's bark behind him.

Rain soaked Karl's face with each step outside. The boards in his arms pinched his skin as they shifted. He scanned the yard in front of him, his shotgun swinging from his shoulder.

He needed a dry place. He wasn't sure why, but it needed to be dry. He saw the damp shadows under towering ponderosas, spruces, and hemlocks. He saw the sealed garage door. He saw the shed. He looked into the disused pasture to the west, where in his youth, a horse shelter once shielded Betty, the dun mare. The roof had holes in its ancient tin, but it was largely intact; the dirt below it, mostly dry.

"There," Karl mumbled.

He set off across the driveway, through the dilapidated gate that had been standing open for the past six years. Tall grass, dry to the bone but dripping from rain, brushed his jeans and hissed as it swayed in the breeze. And behind him, the house shook harder.

Karl paused under the shelter. He glanced back at the house, where the beast seemed still within the doorway. Brady barked–was he holding it back? The home's roof rattled. The walls creaked, and Karl noticed the shingles raising, peeling backward toward the sky.

Crack. The house screamed.

Karl was frozen as he imagined what might come next. What was it going to do? To the house? To him? He saw the thing's tentacles grip the doorway and thrust the monster through.

Crack. The doorjamb burst into shards. Raging black smoke swirled and rotated in the rain.

He wondered about the shotgun. Should he shoot it? It was too far away; that wouldn't have any effect. He needed to continue–to make the symbols work.

Karl ripped his gaze from the beast.

Crack.

He began arranging the wood on the ground. There was a circle in his dream. A circle would work here. It had to. He placed the pieces from the left and right sides of the cabinet on the left and right of an open space in the dirt.

Crack.

He placed two pieces from the cabinet's back at the top. One was fractured, but he squeezed the wood back together, joining the symbol's broken marks.

Crack.

He placed the final one, from the front left door, on the bottom left of his circle. It was the last thing he had, and one symbol was missing. *Shit.* He knew it was missing but did this anyway. He wanted to smack himself in the face.

Boom. It was like a bomb. The sound behind him shook his bones. He had to turn–the thing was coming. It was coming, and it would kill him.

Karl stood and ripped the stone from his pocket. He held it over the center of his arrangement and prayed, "Let this work. God, please let this work."

Through the rushing wind and the downpour, through the ting and clang of the water against the tin roof, he heard it coming. The beast stormed across the ground, dragging its limbs and roaring over the storm.

He dropped the disc and turned away. It had to work. No matter what bullshit he had done wrong in life, this had to work. No matter what bad was in this world, it deserved to live without this monster. No matter how bad of a father he had been, he had to do this last part right and save Amanda.

The disc smacked the earth with a thump, raising a cloud of dust as large as it. For a half-second, time stood still in Karl's mind. He waited for a miracle–for the ring with a missing symbol to work–despite knowing otherwise.

He was doomed. His daughter was doomed. This thing would rip into him and leave only strings of flesh behind. It would tear her apart. He saw it moving across the world, destroying and eating whatever came into its path, and there was nothing he could do.

Karl fought through the cold chill of certain death that wrapped his frame. He raised the shotgun from underneath his arm and pointed it at the incoming cloud–the flailing claws of death. He squeezed the trigger and heard almost nothing. The weapon's stock slammed into his shoulder. It felt numb as flame and smoke exploded from the barrel.

A hole burst through the center of the oncoming thing. Black smoke, black blood, and chunks of tendril meat flew. But it kept coming.

Karl swore he heard a laugh inside his head. It was mocking him.

Tentacles swung and popped, whipped and cracked. The unholy thing was just across the driveway. Its reach was halfway there, and Karl knew his time was short.

He pumped the shotgun, aimed dead center of the ball of smoke, and fired. Smoke blew away but more swirled to fill it in. Black blood spilled, but slowed it none. It crossed the parking pad and entered the pasture.

Karl pumped again. He aimed at the closest writhing arms.

Boom. It splattered into black meat, retreated inside the smoke, and was replaced by another–this one bearing fanged jaws.

He pumped again and aimed at the next closest, only ten feet away.

Boom. The pasture grass was stained by an onyx blob. Another fang-mouthed tentacle raced to take its place.

This was useless. It was getting worse, and he only had one shot left.

Karl pumped. He aimed at the beast, his hands shaking. Where to shoot? He tried the center. He tried the arms. What was left? What would actually make a difference?

A snapping mouth flew at Karl. There was no more thought. Whether it was the right shot or not, it was what he had to do. He aimed at the incoming tentacle and squeezed the trigger.

Boom. Fangs, flesh, and all vaporized from the last three feet of the limb. It seemed to squeal as it retracted back into the cloud.

Karl had but seconds to record his temporary glee at the amazing shot, then two clawed tentacles seized his leg. It wasn't until they yanked him from his feet that he felt the searing rip of its barbs inside his flesh. It was like a thousand burning fish hooks digging into his skin and muscle, diving toward bone and dragging him away.

Karl screamed.

The jaw-faced arm clamped down on Karl's left wrist and pulled. Another claw-tipped tendril hooked around his waist, and Karl thought it was digging for his intestines as it crushed him from all sides.

Karl howled again. He screamed in ways he never knew he could, in a pitch and volume that rattled his eardrums.

"No!" was all he could articulate as he slid across the ground to the endlessly cycling, gaseous thing.

This was it. This was the end. He thought of Amanda, and shame washed over him. He couldn't protect her. He glanced at the Jeep. There she was, watching him through the rear window. And she would be next.

Karl's eyes rolled from the pain. He knew he was only inches from the beast and fought to open them one more time, to take one last glimpse of the world before it was all gone.

His eyes fell on the horse shelter. He had to wonder for a split-second if what he was seeing was real and decided it was. Brady was there, standing over the ring of symbols. He glowed a gentle blue that lit the shelter's interior, and his paw was in the empty spot where the symbol was missing. And it looked like he was drawing in the dirt.

A scream filled the dusk. Karl thought it was himself, then realized it was coming from the cloud. The tentacles that grasped him vibrated. Their barbs ripped his skin as they shuffled forward and back. The mouth released. The arms tore themselves away, taking chunks of Karl's flesh with them. Karl flopped to the grass and caught just a glimpse as each tentacle zipped into the cloud, and the cloud sucked itself into a pinpoint of black–and snapped out of existence–*pop*.

Karl inhaled into a painful chest. He exhaled carefully as his skin shrieked from the hundreds of holes. His gaze circled the pasture, the house, the Jeep. Was this real? Had the thing really gone? And his view fell onto the horse shelter once again, where Brady sat beside a finished ring and guarded it.

CHAPTER SEVEN

There wasn't a lot of time before the police came. Enough for Karl and Amanda to find a shoebox inside his closet, transfer the strange symbols to its sides, drop the stone disc into it, and bury it behind the horse shelter inside a garbage bag.

They showed up and threw Karl to the ground. His blood streamed all over them through still unbandaged wounds. They mentioned an ambulance, but decided it wasn't that bad, and instead, drove the father and daughter to the hospital. She hugged him as he bled. He tried to ignore the pain and stored away this memory–who knew how long he'd be in jail for, possibly life as he saw it.

After Amanda was seen by the doctor, and the officer in charge found out Suzanne was too drunk to drive, they took the girl home.

Karl had a much longer night. He was sewn up–it took hours. Over three-hundred stitches. He was interrogated until what felt like morning. After it finally seemed like it was over for now and they'd shown him to his cell, the lead detective asked him one more time, "Why'd you do it? Why'd you kill them?"

It sunk into his brain like a brick in Lake Big Horn, he was never going to be a free man again. He wished he could tell them the truth, point them to the box and show them. But he knew if he did, that thing would probably get free forever. He'd have to settle for this. For saving their lives silently, even if they'd never know it.

They moved him from the interrogation room to a cell, one of four at the Custer Falls City-County Building. He laid on his cot and thought of the one good thing. The box was buried beside Brady, and that dog would keep it safe as long as he could.

ABOUT THE AUTHOR

D.W. Hitz lives in Montana, where the inspiring scenery functions as a background character in his work. He is a lover of stories in all mediums. He enjoys writing in the genres of Horror, Supernatural/Paranormal Thriller, and Science Fiction/Fantasy.

Originally from Norfolk, VA, D.W. has degrees in Recording Arts and Web Design and Interactive Media. He has been a creative his entire life. This creativity has driven him in writing, music, and web design and development. He aspires to tell stories that thrill the heart and stimulate the imagination.

When not writing, D.W. enjoys spending time with his family, hiking, camping, and playing with the dogs.

www.DWHitz.com

WHAT'S NEXT?

D.W. Hitz is always hard at work creating new stories. Stay tuned for more content coming soon.

More great speculative fiction is in the works at Fedowar Press. Check out the following titles coming soon.

More on https://www.FedowarPress.com.

Printed in Great Britain
by Amazon